ANIMAL
RESCUE CENTER

The
Homeless
Foal

ANIMAL MAGIC

ANIMAL
°✚RESCUE CENTER

Other titles in the series:

ANIMAL
RESCUE CENTER

The Homeless Foal

by TINA NOLAN

tiger tales

tiger tales

5 River Road, Suite 128, Wilton, CT 06897
Published in the United States 2017
Originally published in Great Britain 2007
by Little Tiger Press
Text copyright © 2007, 2017 Jenny Oldfield
Interior illustrations copyright © 2017 Artful Doodlers
Cover illustration copyright © 2017 Anna Chernyshova
Images courtesy of www.shutterstock.com
ISBN-13: 978-1-58925-498-5
ISBN-10: 1-58925-498-8
Printed in China
STP/1800/0114/0816

For more insight and activities, visit us at www.tigertalesbooks.com

This series is for my riding friend Shelley,
who cares about all animals.

ANIMAL MAGIC
RESCUE CENTER

 HOME

 ADOPT

 FRIENDS

MEET THE ANIMALS IN NEED OF A HOME!

BRUNO

A yellow Labrador, about four years old, Bruno is a wonderful dog who likes people.

LOTTIE

This 2-year-old Scottie is a bundle of fun! Lottie loves children and would like to come out to play!

SUGAR AND SPICE

Kittens Sugar and Spice are adorable! They're ready to go to new owners and would like a home together.

SITE SEARCH

 NEWS

 HELP US

 CONTACT

 DONATE!

JOEY

Joey the greyhound is too old to race. He would love a comfy, quiet home where he can dream of rabbits!

PRINCE

An active and energetic Dalmatian with plenty of character. Can you keep up with this playful dog?

SALT AND PEPPER

Two more sweet kittens are looking for a friendly new home. Can you step in and give them the love they need?

Contents

Chapter One

Rescuing Tigger

"Almost there!" Ella called to her brother, Caleb.

Caleb was climbing a tree to rescue Tigger, a tabby cat who had managed to get himself stuck.

"Climb to your right—a little more," Ella instructed. "Yes, now try!"

Caleb eased himself along the branch and reached out with one hand.

"Be careful!" Tigger's owner, Miss Elliot, warned. She held her hands to her mouth, hardly daring to look.

"That's it. You're almost there."
Jimmy Harrison, Caleb and Ella's
grandfather, urged his grandson on.

The cat cowered, his yellow eyes
glinting.

"Come here, Tigger!" Caleb called
softly. He stretched as far as he dared.
Down below, Ella, their grandfather,
and Miss Elliot watched anxiously.

"Don't worry," Grandpa told Miss Elliot. "We'll soon have Tigger down."

"That's a good boy," Caleb whispered as the cat stretched out a paw. "Come on, Tigger."

Tigger inched forward, his tail between his legs. Finally, Caleb reached out and grabbed hold of him.

"Yes!" Ella cried, as Caleb clasped the cat to him and began to climb down.

"Oh, my!" Miss Elliot gasped, smiling with relief.

Grandpa grinned at his elderly neighbor. "I told you Caleb could do it! Now all you have to do is give that cat his dinner. And while you're at it, could you please put the kettle on for a nice cup of tea?"

As their grandfather and Miss Elliot

disappeared inside the big house, Ella welcomed Caleb and Tigger back to the ground. "Nice one!" she grinned at her brother, taking the cat from him while he brushed himself off.

"Animal Magic at your service, ma'am!" he laughed.

"Yeah, whatever. Anyway, I'm glad Grandpa thought to call us. Miss Elliot was about to call the fire department!"

"Hmmm…. It's good that Grandpa lives next door," Caleb muttered. Looking up at Miss Elliot's big house, Caleb could see paint peeling from the window frames and ivy choking the broken gutters. "This is one gigantic house for an elderly lady living by herself."

Ella nodded, then carried Tigger

indoors. "Who's hungry?" she asked.

The second he saw his food dish, Tigger leaped out of her arms. Soon he was munching happily.

"Thank you so much," Miss Elliot told Ella and Caleb. "It's a relief to have Tigger back safe and sound."

Ella and Caleb blushed. Their grandfather smiled proudly.

"Now I know why your rescue center is called Animal Magic," Miss Elliot said, shedding a happy tear. "It's as if I waved a magic wand and you gave Tigger and me a happy ending. We simply can't thank you enough!"

"Okay, Bruno, lie still while I take a look at you." Heidi Harrison, Ella and

Caleb's mom, spoke gently to the yellow Labrador on her examination table.

Ella and Caleb had raced back from Miss Elliot's house and burst into their mom's operating room, eager to tell her the exciting Tigger rescue story.

The injured dog whimpered and stared up at Mom with his deep brown eyes.

Joel Allerton, Mom's assistant, stood close by. "Slow down," he said. "This poor fellow has had a nasty fall. He was found at the foot of a 20-foot-high wall. It looks like he tore a ligament."

Carefully, Mom tested the movement in Bruno's shoulder joint. "Yes," she confirmed. "He's probably going to need surgery to fix it."

"What happened? Did somebody dump him?" Ella asked.

Joel nodded.

"Your dad found him on the outskirts of town, where the railway bridge crosses the road. We think he got pushed over the edge and landed on the grass below."

"Will he be okay?" Suddenly their exciting story about rescuing Tigger didn't seem as important.

Her mom nodded. "He should be fine. He's very lucky. There's a name tag on his collar, but no phone number. He's not microchipped, either, so it'll be hard to find the owner."

"Poor Bruno!" Ella said. Inside, she boiled with anger over the idea that anyone could shove this beautiful dog off a bridge. She stood back as Joel prepared a painkilling injection.

The dog whimpered again and raised his head.

Caleb frowned. "Should I enter him on the website?" he asked.

"Yes, go ahead and put his details up," Mom said. She took the syringe from Joel and rubbed Bruno's ears. "'Yellow Lab, male, about four years old. A beautiful dog who likes people.'"

Nodding, Caleb disappeared into the office and sat at the computer. He typed quickly, then came back to take a photo of Bruno to put on the site.

"Where's Dad?" Ella asked.

"Outside, putting the finishing touches to the stables," her mom told her. "Can't you hear him hammering?"

Yes, the stables! The very word cheered Ella up.

Animal Magic was about to open its doors to bigger unwanted animals such as horses, ponies, and goats, in addition to the dogs, cats, and rabbits they already took care of. A team of volunteers had given up their time to convert a cowshed in the corner of the old barnyard. By this time next week, the stables would be ready.

"I'll go and help!" she decided, heading out of the operating room and across the yard to join her dad.

Chapter Two
Animal Magic Under Threat

All that evening and the next day, Ella
worked in the new stables with her dad.
She used a screwdriver to fix bolts on
doors, and a hammer to nail planks of
wood to a partition wall.

"Good job," her dad told her before
he left for work the following morning.
"Tonight I'll pick up the bales of straw
I ordered from Tom Larsen's farm. You
can come with me if you'd like."

"Yes, please." Ella always enjoyed a

visit to Tom's place. High Trees Farm was on the edge of town, and Tom owned the fields at the back of Animal Magic.

Ella continued to hammer. "How's Bruno?" she asked Joel when he poked his head over the stable door.

"Surgery went well," Joel replied. "The shoulder should heal in a few days."

"That's great news." Ella knew that Caleb had already taken two inquiries about Bruno on the website. "At this rate, we'll get him better and find him a new home before the end of spring break."

"Another success story," Joel grinned. "We're working our magic…"

"…to match the perfect pet…"

"…with the perfect owner!" Joel and Ella chanted the Animal Magic slogan.

Ella put down her hammer and stood

back. "Time for a break," she decided.

"Do you want to come with me to pick up our bulk order of cat food from Norris Farm Supply?" Joel asked.

"Sure! I'll let Mom know." She followed him out to the yard, trying to sneak past Mrs. Brooks next door without attracting attention.

But Linda Brooks looked up from planting a neat row of red and white flowers along the side of her lawn.

"Is Annie having a good time in Ashton?" Ella asked about her friend who was on vacation with her cousins.

"Fine, thank you, Ella," came the brisk reply.

Mrs. Brooks peeled off her gardening gloves and came up to the wall. "Joel, I'd like a word with you if you can spare a moment."

"Sure. What can I do for you, Linda?"

"You can pass on a message, please. I'd like you to tell Heidi to expect a visit from the Council."

Joel and Ella exchanged worried looks.

"Jason and I have lodged our petition at the Town Hall," Mrs. Brooks explained. "We gathered signatures of people opposing Animal Magic on the grounds of excess animal noise and car traffic, and I delivered the petition to the Council office on Monday morning."

"Good for you, Linda," Joel muttered under his breath.

Ella could hardly bear to listen. *This*

is the countryside! she thought. *Animals live in the country. You expect them to make noise!* She couldn't believe that Annie's parents had actually gone ahead and done what they'd been threatening to do ever since Animal Magic started up a year earlier.

"So you'll inform Heidi?" Linda asked stiffly. Joel nodded. Mrs. Brooks gave a triumphant smile before turning on her heel and going back to her gardening.

Joel sighed and hung his head. "Come on, Ella. Forget the cat food for now," he muttered. "I'd better pass this news on to your mom before I lose control and leap over that fence to tear up Linda's precious flowerbed!"

"I've been expecting it," Mom admitted when Ella and Joel gave her Mrs. Brooks's message. She was in an exam room, busy with a new arrival—a cat that was still inside a cat carrier, meowing to be let out.

"Mrs. Brooks is so mean!" Ella cried. "She's asking the Council to close us down without even thinking about what will happen to all of our animals if they do!"

"I know." Mom had gotten used to her neighbor's constant complaints and threats. Even now she was determined not to let it upset her. "Let's not think about that now, Ella. Why don't you open up the carrier and help me take a look at this little fellow."

"What if Animal Magic has to close?" Ella asked worriedly, unhooking the latch on the carrier. "Where will all our animals go?"

"Not now, Ella. Joel, we'll need to open a new unit in the cat area. Can you go and make sure there's food and water?" Ella opened the carrier and her mom reached inside, lifting out a wary tabby cat with staring yellow eyes.

"Hey, that's Tigger!" Ella recognized him right away. She ran to the door and called for Caleb, who was busy cleaning his bike in the yard. "Caleb, come here.

Miss Elliot's tabby has been brought in!"

"What happened?" Caleb asked, his forehead damp under his floppy, dark hair. He'd just ridden his bike to Crystal Park and back with his friend George Stevens.

"Hey, Tigger!" Ella whispered, petting his soft, striped fur. "What happened to Miss Elliot?" she asked her mom.

"Go ask Grandpa," Mom answered, beginning to examine the new arrival. "He brought Tigger in half an hour ago."

"Let's ride our bikes over there," Caleb said in a hurry, hardly waiting for Ella to grab her bike and follow.

Ella and Caleb sped along Main Street, toward their grandfather's garden center on the edge of Crystal Park. Soon they saw the large green and white Gro-Well sign and the long rows of greenhouses where Grandpa grew (and sold) his plants.

"Grandpa, why did you bring Tigger to the rescue center?" Caleb asked, charging into the store.

Ella was right behind him. "What happened to Miss Elliot? Is she okay?"

Grandpa, who was potting small green seedlings into larger pots, looked over the rim of his glasses. "Ah, yes. Not good news, I'm afraid," he replied. "I found poor Miss Elliot collapsed on her kitchen floor this morning. I had to call for an ambulance."

"Did she go to the hospital?" Ella gasped.

Her grandfather nodded. "I don't know how long she'll be there, but she asked me to take care of her animals."

28

Caleb fiddled with the plastic plant labels on the counter. "Animals—plural?"

"I thought Tigger was the only one," Ella cut in.

"Tigger is the only *cat*," her grandpa agreed. "And it was easy enough for me to drop him off at your place."

"But?" Caleb prompted.

"But Buttercup is more of a problem," Grandpa said. "I've already called your dad, and he's going over there as soon as he can."

"Buttercup?" Ella stared at the tall, gray house next door. "Who's she?"

"Come and see," their grandfather invited. He led the way down the side of the greenhouses and through a narrow gate into a field. "I couldn't exactly fit this fine lady into the back of my tiny truck!"

The green field sloped gently toward a stream where a row of willow trees grew. As Ella and Caleb took in the view, they saw a large, gray shape in the shadow of the overhanging branches.

"Wow, is that a pony?" Caleb gasped.

Ella's mouth fell open. Sure enough, a beautiful dapple-gray pony emerged from the trees. Her mane and tail were pure white. She trod heavily up the hill toward them.

"Meet Buttercup," their grandpa announced. "This is Miss Elliot's gray mare. And as you can see, she's about to give birth to a foal any day now!"

Chapter Three

Buttercup's New Home

"She's beautiful!" Ella breathed, watching her dad and grandpa begin to load the gray mare into a trailer that Dad had borrowed from Tom Larsen.

Buttercup's mane was silky soft, and her dappled coat shone in the sunlight.

"Take good care of her," Grandpa said. "Remember, I promised Miss Elliot that her pony would get the royal treatment!"

"Looks like we'll have to open the stables

early," Caleb said. "Should I go ahead and make sure everything's ready?"

His dad nodded. "I dropped off the bales of straw on the way here. Ella, you go with your brother and make a nice deep bed in the stable closest to the door, okay?"

As Caleb rode off, Ella lingered to see her dad lead Buttercup safely up the ramp into the trailer. Then she set off, pedaling hard until she reached home.

"Mom!" she yelled. "Dad's bringing a pony! She's having a foal! We have to lay straw in a stable for her!"

Mom stood in the doorway of the animal hospital. "I know. Caleb already told me. It's exciting, isn't it?"

"Totally. She's beautiful, Mom. Just wait until you see her!" Flinging her bike down, Ella raced into the stable block, where she found Caleb cutting through string that tied the bales of straw. She dived in and took an armful, scattering it on the floor. "How cool is this!"

"Calm down," Caleb grunted. "Look at you—you're covered in straw."

"I don't care. We're getting a pony!" Ella's dark eyes shone. Suddenly, she stared at Caleb. "Hey, do you think the foal will be born while Buttercup's here?"

"It depends how long Miss Elliot has to stay in the hospital," Caleb pointed out.

"The pony did look pretty pregnant, didn't she?" Ella said eagerly.

"Oh, so now you're an expert, huh?" As usual, Caleb tried not to let his feelings show.

"I bet she'll have the foal here!" Ella insisted. "How cool would that be?"

At the sound of their dad's van, they both ran out into the yard. They helped him slide the bolts at the back of the trailer, and then lower the ramp.

"Let's take a look at the mother-to-be," Mom said, coming forward to examine Buttercup before they unloaded her. "Oh, yes, it's going to be any day now. Bring her out gently. Keep her nice and calm."

Ella held her breath as her dad led Buttercup down the ramp. "Her stable's ready," she said, holding the door open.

"Easy, girl," Dad said. He waited for the mare to take in her new surroundings.

She stood in the doorway, looking this way and that. Her ears were pricked, and she swished her tail. Then she must have decided that her new home was good enough, because she stepped forward onto the fresh straw bed and let out a long, satisfied whinny.

"Buttercup needs peace and quiet," Mom told Ella. "When a mare is about to give birth, the last thing she wants is people petting her and hovering."

"But how will we know when it's

happening?" Ella asked.

"We may not. It often happens in the middle of the night, very naturally, without any help from us."

Ella nodded. "So we come out in the morning and the foal is here, already tottering around on its wobbly legs!" She pictured the magical moment.

"Fingers crossed," Mom said. "So what I'm saying is, leave Buttercup alone for a while. How about taking a dog for a walk instead?"

Ella nodded and went to get Prince from the kennels. As she went in she was greeted by a chorus of woofs and barks.

"Hey, Sam, hey, Lottie, hey, Millie," she said as she passed by each kennel, saying hello to a retriever, a Scottie, and a collie.

"Your turn for a walk, Prince," she told the cute Dalmatian.

Prince loved his runs along the riverbank, and when he saw the leash in Ella's hand, he went crazy with excitement.

"Down!" she told him sternly. "Heel!" she said as she got him on the leash.

They left the kennels, crossed the yard, and went down an alley toward the river, where Ella let Prince off the leash.

Off he dashed, sniffing at the entrance to a rabbit burrow, then on through the long grass with just the tip of his white tail showing.

"Prince, come back!" Ella cried, as the playful Dalmatian made a sharp detour over a narrow stone bridge toward the Crystal Park golf course.

Luckily he obeyed and came bounding back to Ella. On the other side of the river, a group of golfers gathered on a smooth green. Ella recognized Jason Brooks, their next door neighbor.

"Heel, Prince!" she said, glad that she and Caleb had spent time training him not to run off. He even ignored the two fishermen sitting on the riverbank, who surprised Ella by standing up and yelling at her to go away.

Ella frowned. She didn't like the look of the two men, who seemed to be angry without good reason.

"Come here, Prince! Heel!" she called again.

Obediently Prince walked to heel, tail and head up, as they headed away from the river, along a footpath beside one of the fields belonging to Tom Larsen. The footpath brought them back onto Main Street, where Ella put Prince on the leash and walked him home. "Good boy!" she said with a grin, thinking that he looked like a pirate, with the big black patch over one eye.

Prince wagged his long tail and trotted into the kennels, where Ella settled him down for the night.

"Good night, Joey, good night, Trixie," she said, passing a greyhound and a Jack Russell.

The dogs yapped and wagged their tails. As Ella turned off the light and closed the door, they fell silent.

She crossed the yard and went into the house to find Caleb at his computer, updating the Animal Magic website.

"Hi, Ella. A woman is coming to look at Prince tomorrow," he reported.

"Cool. Where are Mom and Dad?"

"In their room."

Ella heard the low voices of her parents from across the hall. "The Council is sending someone to see us tomorrow afternoon," Mom was saying. "They didn't give an exact time."

"Do you want me to be here?" Dad asked.

"No, it's only a quick visit. I can tell them everything they need to know."

Ella gasped. "Did you hear that?" she hissed at Caleb, who nodded.

"Let's hope they don't take Linda's side,"

Dad went on. "We could be in serious
trouble if they do." There was a long
pause. "It will mean that all our work
at Animal Magic will have to stop,"
Mom admitted. "The Council could
close us down overnight!"

Ella lay awake late that night worrying.
Every time she closed her eyes she
pictured a man from the Council signing
a piece of paper saying that Animal
Magic had to close.

Then who would find a home for
Bruno once his shoulder had healed, or
for Joey the greyhound who was too old
to race anymore? Who would take care
of animals like Tigger and Buttercup
while their owners were in the hospital?

Ella tossed and turned. It was no good—she couldn't sleep even if it was two o'clock in the morning! Getting out of bed, she crept to her window, opened it, and listened to the silence. In the distance there was the low hoot of an owl.

I wonder how Buttercup is doing, she thought, looking over at the stables. She listened in the darkness, and after a few moments was sure she could hear restless movements coming from the stables—the sound of the pony's feet rustling through dry straw, a low snort, the knock of a hoof against a wooden door. That did it—whatever her mom had said about Buttercup needing peace and quiet, Ella had to go and take a look!

Chapter Four

A Nighttime Delivery

Ella found Buttercup standing in her
bed of straw. She tossed her head in the
low glimmer of a safety lamp fixed high
on the wall.

"Hey, girl!" Ella said. She watched
anxiously as the mare began to pace
to and fro, then folded her knees and
went down on her side, only to get
up and pace again. "Take it easy,"
Ella breathed.

But Buttercup was restless. She rustled

through the straw, went down again, rolled onto her other side and was back on her feet.

"I guess it's time for your foal to be born," Ella whispered, feeling sure she was right. She didn't move.

Buttercup went down on her side a third time, and stayed. Her wide sides heaved as she laid her head on the straw.

"Oh!" Ella was scared. Buttercup looked agitated and helpless. Would it be okay to go into the stall with her?

The mare lifted her head from the straw. She rolled her eyes.

"You're doing fine!" Ella told her.

There were footsteps outside, and Mom came into the stable. "I couldn't sleep either. I heard you come down," she said to Ella. She took one look at the mare. "This is it!"

She went into the stable and knelt down by Buttercup's side to take her pulse. Then she held a stethoscope to the mare's belly. "Uh-oh. The foal's heartbeat isn't very strong. I think Buttercup will need help to deliver it," she decided. "Ella, Joel's on night duty. Run to the animal hospital and get him."

Nodding, Ella ran off. She found Joel
feeding a litter of orphan kittens with
milk from plastic droppers. "Buttercup
… foal … come quick!" she gasped.

Together, they ran back to the stables.

"Okay, this is happening faster than
I expected," Mom warned. "The foal's
head has already emerged. Joel, help
me ease it out, please. Ella, stay where
you are."

Anxiously, Ella watched her mom and
Joel assist Buttercup. She saw the new
foal emerge and slither gently onto the
straw.

"It's over," Mom said, glancing up at
Ella.

"Is she … are *they* okay?" Ella asked.

Mom's eyes shone. "Come and see."

Ella tiptoed toward Buttercup's stall

and peered in.

"I had to turn the foal's head and help him out," Mom said.

Him? The foal was a "he"! Ella held her breath. And there he was—the smallest, youngest, skinniest, shakiest foal she'd ever seen!

The baby lay in the straw. His mother licked him, and then nudged him with her nose. He braced his front legs and tried to push himself up.

"His head is enormous!" Ella exclaimed. "And his legs are so skinny!"

Buttercup nudged and shoved him gently from behind. The foal was gray, like her, with big, dark eyes.

Once more he tried to stand. He got up and tottered, fell over, tried again.

"Wow!" Ella gasped. "How amazing!"

"That's what they're programmed to do," Mom told her quietly. "In the wild, they have to be up on their feet and running away from danger almost the minute they're born!"

And now the foal was standing on his shaky legs, and Buttercup was licking him clean.

"This is so-o-o magical!" Ella breathed. "Buttercup, you're amazing!"

"Would you like to give him a name?"

her mom asked, smiling at Joel.

Ella gazed at the foal. "Let's call him Chance," she whispered. "Because it was only by chance that he came to be born here."

"So, Miss Elliot, you'll be happy to know that your mare has had her foal," Grandpa said.

He had brought Caleb and Ella to visit Miss Elliot in the hospital just after lunch the following day. She looked pale and thin, propped up on pillows, with her sheets folded neatly under her chin.

"He's gray, like his mom," Ella began. "His mane sticks straight up, and he has the longest legs. I was there when he was born!"

"Slow down," Caleb scolded. "I'm sorry. Ella's always cutting in."

Miss Elliot smiled weakly. "No problem at all. You're excited, aren't you, dear? And so am I. I was looking forward to seeing the birth myself, but it wasn't meant to be."

"Chance got up on his feet right away!" Ella exclaimed.

"Chance?" Miss Elliot asked.

Ella blushed. "Oh, Mom said I could give him a name—just for now—so I chose 'Chance.'"

"What a good choice. I think he should keep it. And how is my beautiful Buttercup?"

"Mom says she's doing well," Caleb reported. "And so is Tigger. He's happy in the cat bay."

Miss Elliot nodded, and then turned her head toward Grandpa. "The doctors tell me I had a slight stroke—nothing too serious, but it's given me a shock."

"You'll have to take it easy from now on," Grandpa told her kindly. "When you get back home, I'll pop in and keep an eye on you, don't you worry."

Tears appeared in Miss Elliot's eyes. She shook her head and they trickled down her lined cheeks. "I'm afraid I won't be going home, Mr. Harrison."

"Well, not yet," he conceded. "But in a while, when you're stronger."

"Not ever," she told him faintly. "I have to face facts and admit that the house is too much for me now."

Grandpa was about to protest, but Miss Elliot shook her head.

"I've lived in the old house all my life, and I will always have many wonderful memories of my time there. But I've made up my mind to sell it and move into an apartment," Miss Elliot announced. "Tigger will be able to come with me, but not the ponies, of course."

Ella gasped in alarm. *This can't be happening!* she thought. She stared at Miss Elliot's sad face.

"I would like your son and daughter-in-law to find a wonderful new home for Buttercup and her foal," Miss Elliot insisted. "I would be so grateful to them if they could do that for me."

Chapter Five

An Important Visit

"Buttercup and Chance." Caleb typed the ponies' names on to the Animal Magic website at the reception desk in the animal hospital. He remembered what Miss Elliot had told him. "Mother and foal need to be adopted together. Buttercup trail rides in company and alone at all paces. Good in traffic. Chance needs to be with his mom."

"Hey, Ella," Caleb called. "Does this sound okay?"

She listened carefully as he read the new description. "You've used the word 'need' twice," she pointed out.

"Okay, Miss Fussy, I'll change one of them," Caleb replied, then continued typing. "I'll be out to take photos in a couple of minutes," he muttered. "Can you get Buttercup and Chance ready?"

"What do you mean?" Ella asked.

"You know, brushing and grooming. Horse stuff." Caleb tried to pretend that he didn't know or care much about it, but really he was as much in love with the mare and her foal as everyone else. Every time he looked at Chance, his heart melted.

"Give me five minutes," Ella replied, dashing out to the stables. Once there, she slowed down, moving quietly around

the ponies as she mucked out and laid
fresh straw, and then started to brush
Buttercup's long mane.

The mare stood patiently, keeping one
watchful eye on her foal, who tottered
unsteadily through the new straw.

"He's perfect, isn't he?" Ella whispered,
smiling at Chance's wobbly legs and
soft, fluffy tail. She couldn't believe how
tiny his hooves were, or how big his eyes
and ears seemed. And he wasn't scared
of having her in the stall with them.
Instead, he came close and playfully
nipped at the hem of Ella's T-shirt.

"Hey!" she protested with a smile. She
turned and let him take a good sniff at
her boots and jeans.

Then Buttercup nudged Ella from behind,
as if to say, "You haven't finished yet."

Ella turned back to Buttercup and was just giving her mane a final brush when someone opened the stable door.

"Almost finished," she called, expecting Caleb.

But it was her mom's voice that answered. "Ella, this is Mr. Winters from the Council. He has come to take a look at Animal Magic."

Ella frowned and chewed her lip.
In the excitement of Chance's birth,
she'd forgotten all about Mrs. Brooks's
petition and the visit from the Council.
She mumbled a hello.

"We just opened the stables," Mom
explained to their visitor. "Buttercup
and Chance are our first customers.
I'm hoping to be able to take in goats,
ponies, and donkeys, and I'm planning
to partner with Lucky Star Horse
Rescue to find a permanent place for the
animals that don't get adopted."

"So you don't intend to keep any large
animals here long term?" Mr. Winters
asked. He was a small man, and he wore
a gray suit with a red and gray checkered
tie. He was carrying a blue folder and
seemed to be taking a lot of notes.

Ella continued grooming Buttercup as her mom led Mr. Winters outside.

"No, but we expect this section of the center to be busy, just like the kennels and the cat unit," Mom answered honestly. "In fact, to be frank, Mr. Winters, we're already bursting at the seams."

Ella sighed as the voices faded. She rubbed Buttercup's neck. "You hear that? Mr. Winters is checking up on us to see if we're too noisy."

Buttercup dipped her head and snorted.

"Exactly!" Ella agreed. "That's what I think. And Chance thinks so, too!" She pressed her lips together and made a "puh" sound. *Too noisy? Ridiculous!*

Ella saw Mr. Winters again on his way out. As she came out of the stables, he was shaking hands with her mom, but his face gave nothing away. Was he happy with what he'd seen, or not?

Mom sighed and shook her head as she turned and walked back into the animal hospital. Ella was about to follow when she saw Mrs. Brooks greet Mr. Winters on the driveway.

"Ah, Mr. Winters!" she called. "I'm glad you followed up on my letter of complaint and my petition. Now you can see for yourself how difficult it is for the residents of Crystal Park to have this animal rescue center in our neighborhood!"

Mr. Winters's reply was too low for Ella to hear, but as she stood watching,

Jason Brooks's car pulled into the driveway next door, and Annie jumped out of the back seat.

"Hey, Ella!" Annie cried, dumping her suitcase and running into the yard. "Wow, am I glad to be back! How are you? What's new at Animal Magic?"

"Annie, come and say hi to your mom!" Jason Brooks called in vain. He hurried over to his wife's side just as Mr. Winters was heading to his car.

Annie looked tanned. Her usually neat hair was flying in all directions.

"How was Ashton?" Ella asked.

"Cool. I rode ponies and helped out on the farm every day. But what's happening here? What's with the long face?"

"That was a visit from the Council

to see if your mom can get us closed down!" Ella muttered. But she couldn't stay glum for long. "Forget it. It's not your fault, Annie. And guess what—we have a new foal. Come and look!"

"Annie!" her dad called after her.

"I won't be long!" she yelled as Ella dragged her into the stables.

"Ahhh!" Annie's eyes lit up when she saw Chance.

He was nestled in the deep straw, his long legs folded beneath him. He looked up at the two girls and blinked sleepily.

"How cute is he!" Annie breathed. "Can I go in and pet him?"

Ella nodded. She led Annie into

the stall. "Is this okay?" she asked
Buttercup, who hovered close to where
her foal lay.

The mare lowered her head and made
room for Ella and Annie.

Annie knelt down next to Chance and
reached out to touch him. "He's so soft!"

"He can stand and walk already!"
Ella said, kneeling next to Annie.

Annie could hardly speak through her
broad smile. "What's his name?"

"Chance," Ella whispered.

Annie gave a soft laugh as Chance
nuzzled her hand. "And what's he doing
here at Animal Magic?" she asked.

"He and his mom need a new home,"
Ella explained. "Hey, I don't suppose
you know anyone who lives in a house
surrounded by fields—someone who

loves horses and has room to take in two more?"

Annie sat back. She thought for a while, then answered, "Actually, Ella—I do!"

Chapter Six

A Trip to Lucky Star

"Ashton?" Caleb asked.

The family was discussing Buttercup and Chance's future over dinner that night. Ella had told them about Annie's pony-loving cousins who lived out West.

"I know. They live miles away," Ella said. "But Annie is sure that her aunt and uncle would take them. They already own a horse and a pony."

"But we'd never see them again," Caleb pointed out.

"What's the family's last name?" their
dad asked thoughtfully.

Ella recalled the details that Annie
had given her. "Simmons. There's her
Aunt Ruth and Uncle David, plus
Annie's two cousins, Abby and Mandy.
They live on a farm and have a lot of
space."

"So that must be Linda's sister and
her husband." Mom figured out how
they were related to Mrs. Brooks as she
collected the dirty dishes and put them
in the dishwasher.

Ella traced patterns on the tablecloth
with a fork. "What do you think, Mom?
Is it a good idea?"

Mom turned to Caleb. "Have we
gotten any replies to the ad on the
website?"

He shook his head. "But it's only been up there for a day. Anyway, I think we should say no to Annie's idea—Ashton is too far away."

"I know how you feel, but I think we should check it out," his dad argued. "Look at it from Buttercup and Chance's point of view—a home with other horses and a lot of room to run. It sounds perfect!"

"What else did Annie say?" Mom asked Ella.

"She said her Aunt Ruth and her mom used to ride horses all the time when they were kids. Ruth is still a real animal lover, and Abby and Mandy are, too." Reluctantly, Ella spoke the truth. Like Caleb, she longed to find somewhere closer for Buttercup and Chance.

Frowning moodily, Caleb stood up from the table. "It's a terrible idea. What will Miss Elliot say? She'll have to say good-bye to Buttercup and never see her again. That's not fair!"

"Yeah!" Ella agreed, regretting that she'd mentioned the Ashton thing. She looked from her mom to her dad.

"We need to talk to Miss Elliot," Dad pointed out. "After all, it will ultimately be her decision."

"Meanwhile I'll call Lucky Star Horse Rescue and arrange a visit," Mom said. "You never know—maybe they'll have room for a mare and foal."

"I'll come!" Ella cried, loving her mom's new idea.

"Me, too!" Caleb volunteered.

Please let it be Lucky Star, not Ashton!

Ella wished as she left the house and made a beeline for the stables. *Better yet, let it be Animal Magic forever!*

How cool would that be! Buttercup and Chance could live in Tom Larsen's field at the back of their rescue center. And every morning Ella would get up and go down to the field to see the dapple-gray mare and her handsome foal. They would look up at her and whinny. She would greet them and they would trot through the lush green grass toward her.

She would even buy a saddle for Buttercup and learn to ride. Chance would tag along until he was old enough to be trained....

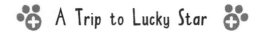
But in her heart Ella knew it wouldn't happen that way. No—Animal Magic would find a new home for the beautiful pair, and Ella's dream would be over.

"Chance is a newborn—he's only a day old," Mom explained to Cathy Brown, the owner of Lucky Star Horse Rescue, the following morning. "We need to find a new home for him. Of course, we won't move him anywhere until he's much older."

"Definitely." Cathy nodded. "And you'll need to find someone who will keep him with his mother for the first year or so, until he's weaned and ready to leave her."

Ella and Caleb sat in the back of their

mom's car, listening to the grown-ups talk. "I like it here!" Ella said.

Caleb grunted. He didn't dare to hope that Lucky Star would become Buttercup and Chance's new home—that would be too good to be true.

"No, honestly—look at all the horses and ponies in the fields!"

Lucky Star sat in a valley with a stream running through it. The yard overlooked three big fields full of grazing animals.

"Fifteen—sixteen—seventeen," Caleb counted. "Twenty-two altogether."

Meanwhile Ella concentrated on Cathy Brown, a tall woman dressed in a blue jacket, jeans, and boots.

"I'm very happy to partner with Animal Magic," Cathy was telling Mom.

"If people bring horses and ponies to me who need a vet, I can bring them to you for treatment. And if you need to find a home for a pony and you've tried everywhere else without success, then I can provide a home here as a last resort."

"Look at that big brown and white one!" Caleb nudged Ella and pointed to a horse that had come up to the gate.

Ella couldn't resist—she got out of the car and went to pet the horse. He had thick, feathery legs and a long white mane that fell forward over his face. He was so hairy that he even had a funny curled mustache at the end of his nose.

"What's his name?" Ella called to Cathy.

"That's Major. He's 33 years old." Cathy came across the yard with a carrot for the elderly horse.

"Wow!" Ella couldn't believe Major's size. "What do you think about Buttercup and Chance?" she asked.

Cathy smiled. "They sound great. And Buttercup sounds like she's a good mother, for sure."

"Chance is so beautiful!" Ella told her.

"And you want to keep him?" Cathy guessed.

Major's mustache wobbled up and down as he ate his carrot.

"Yeah, but we can't," Ella sighed, enjoying the sight of other ponies ambling across the fields toward them. "Can you?" she asked suddenly, keeping her fingers crossed behind her back.

Cathy sighed. "Like I said, Lucky Star is a last resort. And your mom says there's a possibility of Buttercup and

Chance being sent to a good home in Ashton."

"Miles and miles away!" Ella protested.

"But they would do well there—on a farm, with other animals, and kids to ride them."

"*I* could ride them if they lived here," Ella pleaded. She felt her hopes fade as Cathy smiled sympathetically.

"I think they should go to Ashton," Cathy advised. "They'll have a good life there."

Chapter Seven
Love at First Sight

"Okay, so we have two people interested in Buttercup." As soon as they got back from the pony sanctuary, Caleb went into the animal hospital's office and checked the website. "One says she can't take Chance, though."

"We can't split them up!" Ella insisted, reading the emails over her brother's shoulder. "And look, this other one is the opposite—they want the foal but not the mare. What's wrong with them? Don't they read the ads correctly?"

"Hi, Annie. Any news from Ashton?" Mom asked, looking up from her examination of Bruno as Ella's friend appeared.

"Aunt Ruth says she'll definitely think about giving Buttercup and Chance a home," Annie replied cautiously, just as the phone began to ring. "But she can't give an answer right away."

Ella frowned. Right now, with Lucky Star only to be used as a last resort and no other offers coming up, Ashton looked like the only choice.

"Answer the phone, would you please, Ella?" Mom said as she checked the movement in Bruno's injured shoulder.

Ella reached for the receiver.

"Hi, this is Cathy Brown from Lucky

Star," the voice said. "Is this Ella?"

"Yes—do you want to speak to Mom?"

"No, thanks. Can you just pass on a quick message? I forgot to mention one important thing when you came by. The police came here about a week ago to warn me that two horse thieves are operating in the area. I thought you should know, since it'll soon be time to put your mare and foal out to pasture. When you do, make sure the field is secure."

"Okay, thanks." The message worried Ella. For a moment she wondered if the two angry fishermen she'd seen while walking Prince had anything to do with the horse thieves. But when she told her mom, Mom had good news.

"Don't worry. Your dad made a deal

with Tom Larsen earlier today. Tom has
promised to rent us his field facing the
golf course for as long as we need it. You
know, the one you can see from your
house, Annie."

"Hey, cool!" Annie grinned. "I'll be
able to look out of my bedroom window
and see Buttercup and Chance!"

"So?" Ella prompted her mom, trying
not to feel jealous.

"So, there's no direct access to that
field from the main road," Mom
explained. "In other words, no horse
thief can drive a trailer anywhere near
Buttercup and Chance when we put
them out there tomorrow morning."

Reassured, Ella went off with Annie to
feed the kittens in the cat unit. As they
passed by Tigger's pen, Miss Elliot's

tabby gave a loud meow.

"What a beautiful cat!" Annie said.

"He's going back to his owner as soon as she's out of the hospital, so don't get any ideas about adopting him," Ella kidded.

Annie sighed. "Yeah, right! You know what Mom is like!"

"I sure do!" Ella raised her eyebrows. Soon she and Annie were busy with the four tiny kittens, dropping milk into their hungry pink mouths.

The kittens squirmed and swallowed, curling their tongues around the plastic tube and sucking out every drop.

"So, you get to see Chance out of your window and I don't," Ella sighed. Her bedroom overlooked the yard and the animal hospital.

"Yeah, but you got to see him being born!" Annie reminded her. "And you can pet him whenever you like! I can't believe he feels so soft!"

"As soft as these kittens," Ella said. They were finished with the feeding, so she and Annie nestled the kittens down in their warm bed and left the cat bay. "Do you want to take a peek at Chance before you go home?" she asked.

Annie glanced at her watch. "I promised Mom I'd be back at one o'clock—but she won't mind if I'm a few minutes late!"

Ella led the way into the stables. "We need to be very quiet," she whispered.

Chance was resting in the straw. Buttercup raised her head as the girls came close and peered into the stall.

"Oh, he's so cool!" Annie breathed. "And skinny! And cute!"

Ella nodded happily. "Can we come in?" she asked Buttercup, gently opening the door and beckoning Annie in after her. "The first thing I thought after he was born was, 'Wow, he's so skinny!'" she confessed. "Then I saw him stand up on these long, wobbly legs, and I thought he'd never be able to do it, but Buttercup nudged him and he got up and he stood there shaking all over!"

"Is it okay to pet him again?" Annie checked. "Oh, he's so beautiful! Look, he's standing up!"

Jerkily getting to his feet, Chance

shook himself and then tottered toward
Ella. He pushed his soft nose against
her arm, and then gave a small hop and
skip toward Annie.

"He likes me!" Annie smiled. But just
as she reached out to pet him, she heard
her mother's voice calling and getting
closer. "Uh-oh! I should have known!"
With a start she drew back, making
Buttercup glance anxiously toward the
stable door.

"Annie, where are you? I told you not
to be late coming home," Mrs. Brooks
called.

"In here, Mom!" Annie replied softly,
slowly backing out of the stall.

Mrs. Brooks appeared in the door, her
forehead creased by a deep frown. But
when she spotted Buttercup and her tiny

foal, for a moment her face softened.
"Oh, my!" she said, before the hard mask
returned. She cleared her throat. "Annie,
come along. Your lunch is getting cold!"

Blushing, Annie joined her mom, who
sneaked one final look at Chance before
she turned and marched away.

"Did you see that?"
Ella muttered as she patted
Buttercup's neck. "For a second back
there I thought Mrs. Brooks was about
to crack a smile!"

The gray mare nuzzled at Ella's pockets.

"Sorry, no treats!" Ella smiled. "But listen, Buttercup, there was this look on Annie's mom's face, all soft and sweet, like everyone else when they first see Chance. I was so surprised!"

This really made Ella think. She knelt down in the straw beside the foal, who cozied up to be petted. "Of course, she soon switched it off, but I saw it. And you know something?" she added, wrapping her arms around Chance's neck. "The truth is that Mrs. Brooks fell in love with you on the spot."

Chance turned his head and nuzzled Ella's shoulder.

Ella smiled. "She did," she insisted. "And you know something else? I just got an absolutely wonderful idea!"

Chapter Eight

An Outdoor Adventure

"Forget Ashton!" Ella told Caleb, brimming with confidence as she hurried into his room.

Her brother was busy as usual updating the website. He sat with his back to her. "Sugar and Spice are kittens," he typed. "They're ready to go to new owners and would like to find a home together."

"I said, forget Ashton for Buttercup and Chance!" Ella insisted. "I've thought of something terrific!"

"So impress me," Caleb muttered, scanning in an image of the kittens.

"I'm serious, Caleb!" Ella swiveled his chair away from his desk. "You would like to find Chance and Buttercup a home close to Crystal Park, wouldn't you?"

"It's not up to us," he said. "Everyone else thinks Ashton is a good idea."

"Except Miss Elliot!" Ella pointed out. "No one has told her yet, right? It's going to break her heart!"

Caleb frowned. "You're only saying that because you want to keep them nearby so *you* can see them!"

"No, I'm not."

"Yes, you are."

"Well, maybe a little, but do you want to hear my idea or not?"

Caleb turned back toward the screen. "Go ahead. You're going to tell me anyway."

"Okay, this is it! Mrs. Brooks came to get Annie earlier and she saw Chance...."

"Salt and Pepper," Caleb typed, his shoulders hunched, his back to Ella again. "Two more sweet kittens are looking for a friendly new home...."

"Her face softened the moment she saw him!"

"So?"

"So, she's like everyone else—she's fallen in love with him!"

"So?" Caleb muttered again.

"So, she used to go riding when she was young—Annie told me. She loves horses, even if she tries to pretend she doesn't!"

"Are we talking about Linda Brooks, as in the woman who just sent a petition to the Council to get us closed down?" Caleb scoffed.

"Caleb, listen. You didn't see her face when she saw Chance. She really liked him. So my idea is to get Mrs. Brooks to adopt him, along with Buttercup!"

Caleb spun around in his seat, his eyes narrowed. "You're crazy!"

"I am not!"

"Yes, you are. You're always having wacky ideas. Now let me get back to work, okay?"

Ella gritted her teeth. "Just wait and see!" she muttered, flouncing off to her own room. "I'm going to make it happen!"

The next morning, Ella was bringing Joey the greyhound back from a walk by the river when she bumped into Annie at the entrance to Animal Magic.

"Hey, Ella! I was looking for you," Annie greeted her, bending over to pat Joey. "I've got good news. Mom spoke to Aunt Ruth again about Buttercup and Chance, and the answer is yes!"

"Oh!" Ella walked on toward the kennels with Joey.

"Aren't you happy?" Annie ran after her. "Isn't that what you wanted?"

Just then, Ella's grandfather drove through the gates and Caleb came out of the house to say hello.

"How are my favorite grandkids?" Grandpa asked with a broad grin as he got out of his car.

"Grandpa, we're your *only* grandkids!" Ella grinned back, handing Joey's leash to Annie, who had offered to put him back in his kennel.

"Exactly!" He gave her shoulder a quick squeeze. "I thought I'd come and check on Tigger for Miss Elliot."

"How is she doing?" Caleb asked.

"Not too bad. She comes out of the

hospital on Monday, into an apartment building with an on-site super to keep an eye on her. The house is already up for sale."

"Well, tell her Tigger is fine," Caleb said. "And we're pretty sure we've found a home for Buttercup and Chance—in Ashton."

"Yes, it's all set!" Annie announced, coming out onto the porch.

Ella pressed her lips together and kept quiet, watching her grandfather's reaction.

"Well, that's a long way away," Grandpa said, shaking his head. "I'm not sure how Miss Elliot will feel about that."

"She'll hate it!" Ella broke in.

"But it's a good home," Annie insisted.

"I'd better tell Miss Elliot then. I hope it's not too much of a shock," Grandpa said, worried. He set off for the house to find Mom and Dad.

Ella ran after him. "Don't tell Miss Elliot about Ashton just yet," she pleaded.

Her grandfather turned to study her face. "Why? Do you have something else in mind?" he asked.

Ella's eyes were bright and eager. "Actually, yes!" she nodded. "I'm working on it. So don't worry, Grandpa. I'm pretty sure I'll find Buttercup and Chance a place *much* closer to home!"

"Meanwhile, it's business as usual," Mom announced after she and Dad had finished telling Grandpa about the problem with the Council over a cup of coffee.

Ella sat quietly in a corner of the kitchen, listening to their conversation.

"Did they say how long it would take to make a decision?" Grandpa asked.

Dad shook his head. "But you know us, Dad—we always look on the bright side. There are a lot of people in Crystal Park who support Animal Magic, in spite of the ones who signed Linda's petition."

"Why can't people like Linda Brooks see what a good job you're doing here?" Grandpa grumbled.

"Well, we're not solving anything by sitting here and talking," Mom decided, catching Ella's eye. "It's time to take Buttercup and Chance out into the field for the first time. Ella, do you want to put a harness on Buttercup and help me lead her out?"

The words were hardly out of her
mom's mouth before Ella was halfway
across the yard. She dashed into the
stables.

"Guess what!" she told Buttercup,
grabbing a harness from its hook on the
wall. "You're going outside!"

The mare stamped her feet and turned
to edge Chance toward the door.

Carefully Ella strapped the harness
on and clipped a lead rope in place.
"Chance, this will be the first time
you've ever seen the sky and grass
and a river ... and everything!"

The little gray foal gave
a jerky hop,
straight
up in
the air.

"Ready?" Mom asked, appearing at the door. Behind her, Dad, Caleb, and Grandpa held back, curious to see how the new foal would enjoy going out into the field. "Do you want to lead the way?"

Mom opened the door of the stall, and they all moved aside to let Ella and Buttercup pass. Little Chance tottered close behind.

Ella led the procession across the yard and out through a side gate, down a narrow, leafy road and into Tom Larsen's field. Buttercup walked steadily, stopping to snatch a mouthful of fresh green shoots growing in the bushes. Close behind her, Chance sniffed and trotted along.

At last they reached the field. Mom opened the gate and Ella stepped in with Buttercup and Chance.

The tiny foal took his first step onto lush, green grass. He stayed close to his mother at first, following her every step.

Then Chance grew braver. He moved away, taking a sniff here and a sniff there. He looked up at the vast blue sky. He tried out a small skip and a jump.

Buttercup kept a wary eye on him as he ventured out into the big wide world.

Hey, I can jump and I can run! Chance seemed to say. *My legs are like springs! The air smells fresh and good!*

"Look at that!" Ella said, sitting on top of the gate as Chance took another run and a jump. He toppled and fell to the ground, got up again, and trotted back to his mother.

"Adorable!" Mom sighed.

Caleb, Dad, and Grandpa leaned

against the gate, grinning.

Ella watched Buttercup check that Chance was okay before letting him go off to explore again. Then she glanced at the houses overlooking the field. She could see the back of the animal hospital, with its low roof and small windows, and next to it, the Brookses' tall, white house.

"Look, he's getting braver!" Caleb exclaimed, as Chance made his unsteady way up the hill, away from the river toward the houses.

Ella saw the curtain move in a window of the Brookses' house. She glimpsed Mrs. Brooks's face.

Yes! she thought. *Mrs. Brooks is secretly watching! I knew it. I don't care what Caleb says—my plan is going to work!*

Chapter Nine
The Horse Thieves

"Hey, Ella, guess what!" It was
Wednesday evening, and Annie came
looking for her friend in the cat bay.
"I just caught Mom sneaking a peek
at Chance when she should have been
vacuuming!"

Ella gave a broad smile as she tucked
Spice back into the basket alongside her
brothers and sisters. "Tell me more."

"Mom was upstairs vacuuming the
bedrooms. I was downstairs, and I heard

everything go quiet. So I snuck upstairs and found her standing at the window, just staring at Chance in the field."

"Awesome! It's working!" Ella grinned. She decided it was time to let Annie in on her plan. "Annie, my idea is to find a home for Buttercup and Chance really close by. I know your Aunt Ruth would take them, but I was thinking of somewhere *much* closer than Ashton."

"How much closer?" Annie asked.

"So close that they wouldn't have to move at all!" Ella grinned. "My idea is to get your mom to fall in love with Chance so she'll want to adopt him and Buttercup."

"When did you think of that?" Annie gasped.

"A few days ago. It was you who gave

me the idea—when you said that your mom used to love horses when she was a kid."

"Yeah, I know, but…," Annie shrugged. "I guess it might work. But Aunt Ruth already said yes, and Mom isn't the type to back down easily. Remember how she feels about Animal Magic."

"Come into the stables and help me muck out," Ella suggested, guiding Annie across the yard. "People change their minds," she pointed out, handing Annie a shovel. She grinned again at the idea of Mrs. Brooks gazing down at the little gray foal today, his fourth day in the sunny field. "And now that you know the plan, Annie, you have to work on your mom."

"How?"

"Tell her about Miss Elliot never seeing
Buttercup again if she goes to Ashton.
Remind her how beautiful horses are, how
much you'd like to have one because then
you could learn to ride like she did when
she was younger—all that kind of stuff."

Shovel in hand, Annie promised to try.
"But don't hold your breath," she warned.

"Try!" Ella insisted, finishing the work in the stable and picking up Buttercup's harness. "Time to bring them in from the field. Do you want to come?"

Together the girls left the yard by the side gate and went down the path. Everything was calm and quiet as usual, until Ella heard the sound of a car engine in the distance. "That's weird," she muttered, hurrying to the gate and spotting Buttercup and Chance at the far side of the field.

Annie ran after her. "What is?"

"There's no way in for traffic, but I'm sure I just heard a car."

Sure enough, as she climbed the gate into Tom Larsen's field, Ella saw a pickup truck and trailer crossing the old stone bridge over the river. It had driven straight across the empty golf course, heading for the ponies' field.

"That's not right!" she whispered, as alarm bells began to ring in her head.

Hadn't Cathy Brown warned them about horse thieves in the area? And hadn't she herself seen two angry strangers supposedly fishing on the riverbank? "Oh, no!" she cried, taking off running. She had a vision of the two men loading Buttercup and Chance into their trailer and driving off at top speed.

To Ella's surprise, she wasn't the first person to have spotted the pickup truck. Mrs. Brooks had climbed her fence and was sprinting down the field toward the bridge.

The pickup towed the trailer over the

bridge into the field.

"Stop!" Mrs. Brooks called. "This is private property! Leave the pony and her foal alone!"

Frightened by the disturbance, Buttercup and Chance cantered off to the farthest corner of the field.

"They're horse thieves," Ella cried, beginning to panic. "We have to try and catch Buttercup!" She ran across the field, determined to beat the thieves to it, hoping that the sight of Mrs. Brooks waving her arms and yelling would be enough to make them turn around.

The pickup came to a stop, and two burly men stepped out.

"Turn around or I'll call the police!" Mrs. Brooks insisted, going right up to the men. "You have no business being

here. The golf course is private, and this
field is most certainly not a right of way!"

The men folded their arms and stood
with their feet wide apart, taking in the
panicky scene.

"Hey, Buttercup, it's okay," Ella said
softly as she approached the mare. At
her side, little Chance trembled and
peered out from behind her. "We won't
let anything bad happen." Slowly she
slipped the harness on.

Meanwhile, Mrs. Brooks stood her
ground. "Didn't you hear me? I said I'll
call the police."

"And tell them what?" one of the
men asked, the corners of his mouth
twitching as he tried not to smile. "That
Tom Larsen sent us to set up some
electric fencing?"

Mrs. Brooks stared. "Tom Larsen?"

The man nodded. "He's our boss. The fence posts are in the trailer if you'd like to take a look."

"Fence posts?" Taking a deep breath, Mrs. Brooks walked around the back of the trailer and peered inside. "I thought … I mean … I was watching from my window … I thought you were trespassing. And the girls here—they said you were horse thieves!"

"You can't be too careful," the man agreed. "I'm Dan. And this is Nathan. Nathan, get Tom on the phone so he can tell Mrs. …"

"…Brooks," she mumbled. She was red and hot, with beads of sweat forming on her forehead.

"Get him to tell Mrs. Brooks that we are who we say we are."

"That won't be necessary," Mrs. Brooks stammered, calling to Annie and Ella that everything was okay. "I'm awfully sorry. You must think I'm completely silly!"

Slowly Ella led Buttercup and Chance toward the men with the trailer. Chance trotted calmly beside Annie.

Dan grinned. "I feel sorry for any poor horse thief who tries to steal those two. With you three around, they wouldn't stand a chance!"

Mrs. Brooks's blushes deepened. "Annie, Ella, meet Dan and Nathan," she said. "They work for Tom Larsen."

Ella gulped. Annie groaned. But the two men chuckled and said they would come back to do the fencing some other time, when the field was empty. Then they climbed into the pickup truck and drove slowly away.

"Oh, wow!" Ella muttered.

At his mother's side, Chance suddenly took a little skip and hop toward Mrs. Brooks.

"Ahhh!" Annie sighed.

As Ella looked on, she noticed Caleb dashing across the field toward them.

"What happened?" he called. "Why did Mr. Larsen's men drive off without doing their job?"

Ella, Annie, and Mrs. Brooks stared at him.

"You knew about Dan and Nathan?" Ella stammered.

Caleb nodded. "I took a phone call from Mr. Larsen earlier this afternoon. He said to expect his men to show up to set up some electric fencing."

"Thanks for telling us!" Ella groaned.

"Uh-oh. Why do I get the feeling that my little sister just jumped to the wrong conclusion as usual?" Caleb laughed.

"I'm afraid we all did," Mrs. Brooks confessed. She petted Chance and smiled as he hopped a little closer. Then he stuck out his nose and nuzzled her hand.

"Oh, how awful it would have been if those men really had been horse thieves!" Mrs. Brooks sighed. Gently

she petted the foal's soft nose. She went
down on one knee and rested her cheek
against his neck. "You're beautiful!"
she whispered. "I'm sorry if we scared
you, but I thought those men were
coming to steal you, and I couldn't let
that happen!"

Annie nodded at Ella, who smiled
back.

"You're so handsome!" Mrs. Brooks
exclaimed. She looked up at Ella with a
tearful face. "What's his name?"

"Chance," Ella replied.

"It's the perfect name,"
Mrs. Brooks
whispered. "I
feel so lucky
to have met
you, Chance."

Chapter Ten

A Dream Come True

"So you see, we think it would be a wonderful idea if Buttercup and Chance could stay in Crystal Park," Mrs. Brooks told Mom and Dad.

She'd come over to the house with Annie late on Wednesday evening, just as Grandpa had arrived with Miss Elliot to pick up Tigger.

The farmhouse kitchen was full of visitors, all drinking coffee around the big wooden table. Annie sat next to Ella and Caleb with an enormous grin on her face.

Dad cleared his throat. "Let me get this straight, Linda. Are you actually offering a home to the pony and her foal?"

Mrs. Brooks nodded. "I've talked with my sister, Ruth, and she agrees it's by far the best solution to keep them here. I've also spoken to Tom Larsen, who's perfectly happy to keep renting us the field at the back of our house. And of course Jason agrees that it will be wonderful for Annie to have a pony."

"Whoa!" Dad said, holding up both hands. "Did I miss something?" he whispered to Ella.

The shock waves of Mrs. Brooks's offer allowed Miss Elliot to break into the conversation. "Oh, it would be wonderful to be able to visit Buttercup!" she sighed. "It softens the blow of having to sell my house if I know I can still see my beautiful pony!"

"And her new foal!" Ella added. She had a warm glow in her stomach, knowing that Animal Magic had once more done its work to match the perfect pet with the perfect owner.

"Well, Annie, there's no need to ask how you feel about the arrangement!" Ella's mom smiled. "I can tell by the look on your face that you think you're in heaven."

"Pinch me, someone!" Annie sighed. "I'm actually going to have my own pony. Ella, as this is all because of you, you can ride Buttercup whenever you want!"

"Now someone has to pinch me and make me believe what's happening!" Ella exclaimed, closing her eyes and picturing herself riding Buttercup by the river, with Chance trotting along at their side.

Mom turned back to Mrs. Brooks. "And does this mean you'll be withdrawing your petition to have us closed down?"

An embarrassed frown appeared on Mrs. Brooks's face. "I'm afraid it's too late for that. Mr. Winters told me that he's in the middle of writing his report."

"So we'll have to wait and see." Dad nodded.

"Oh, dear, oh, dear," Miss Elliot said softly. "I had no idea!"

"Do you want to come and see Chance?"

Ella cut in, eager to change the subject. She, Annie, and Caleb led Miss Elliot out to the stables. The others followed behind.

There, in the glow of the lamp, Buttercup stood guard over her foal. She raised her head and whinnied as Miss Elliot approached.

"Who's my beautiful girl!" Miss Elliot sighed. Then she gazed down at Chance. "What a handsome little foal you are!"

Chance looked up from his bed of straw. He was too sleepy to get up, although he raised his head and flicked his ears toward the visitors.

"Wonderful!" Miss Elliot whispered with tears in her eyes.

Caleb stood with his hands in his pockets, trying not to let anyone see the tear that had formed in the corner of his eye. Ella felt her own eyes well up with tears. Buttercup and Chance would never be more than a stone's throw from Animal Magic. It was a dream come true.

Annie couldn't help it—she burst out crying in front of everyone. "I'm just so-o-o happy!" she sniffed.

And Chance settled down in his warm bed and slept.

There's always
something going on
at Animal Magic.
Turn the page
for a sneak peek!

Have you read...

ANIMAL RESCUE CENTER

The Unwanted Puppy

Available now!

by TINA NOLAN

Chapter One

"Come here, Copper! Bailey, lie down!"
Ella Harrison yelled at the two Jack
Russell puppies who were scampering
along the riverbank.

The puppies ignored her and ran on
through the long grass, wagging their
pointed tails. "Yip-yap! Yap-yap-yap!"

Ella groaned and dashed after them.
She grabbed Copper before he could stick
his head down a rabbit hole, and then
dragged Bailey out of the shallow water.

"Bad dogs!" she scolded.

Her brother, Caleb, stood on the bridge and grinned. "Bad dogs!" he mimicked. "Face it, Ella, you're lousy at this dog-training stuff!"

The Jack Russells wriggled and squirmed in her arms as she joined Caleb. She frowned at him. "Yeah, well, we're a rescue center, not a dog-training school. And anyway, if you're so good at it, where's Lady right this second?"

Lady was the Border collie he was supposed to be retraining. The dog was

hyper—always jumping up on people and running away. Her owner had dumped her at the Animal Magic Rescue Center, and it had been Caleb's idea to teach her good manners.

"Um...." Caleb looked along the riverbank. "I saw her a second ago. She was down there, playing with a stick."

"Oh! Isn't that her on the golf course?" Ella asked sweetly, pointing at a black-and-white collie charging across the smooth greens, jumping up at golfers, and then racing toward the rescue center.

"Uh-oh!" Caleb set off after the runaway while Ella giggled. She put her two puppies on leashes and followed more slowly, knowing that it was dinnertime and Lady would be heading for home.

But not before the young dog had bounded off the golf course onto the main street, raided a garbage can by the bus stop, and then rampaged through the Brookses' yard, next door to Animal Magic.

"Uh-oh!" Caleb said again, as he spotted Lady digging up their neighbor's lawn.

Ella held Bailey and Copper on tight leashes and ducked behind a bush.

"Shoo!" a high voice shouted. "Get away, you bad dog!"

"Oh, no, that's Annie's mom," Ella whispered to Copper and Bailey, who strained at their leashes, desperate to chase after Lady. "Mrs. Brooks is going to be in a major bad mood over this!"

Caleb dashed through the gate to catch Lady. "Heel, Lady!" he shouted, but to no effect. The collie stopped digging and ran off. She trampled through Mrs. Brooks's bed of bright red tulips.

"Uh-oh!" Ella reported the latest. "Now Lady has wrecked her flowers!"

Fed up with waiting, Bailey and Copper began to yap.

"Shhh!" Ella warned, while Caleb dived after Lady and chased her through Mrs. Brooks's roses.

Just then, as Ella waited with the

terriers on the pavement outside the Brookses' yard, her dad, Mark Harrison, drove up on his way home from work in his van. He leaned out of the window. "Trouble?" he asked.

Ella nodded, pushing her heavy hair back from her hot face. "Lady ran away!" she explained, struggling to hold the Jack Russells back.

"Come on, follow the van," Dad said quickly. "I'll park the van, then come back here to sort things out."

In a flash, Ella did as she was told. "See!" she said to Copper and Bailey, as her dad eased the van in through the gates of the rescue center. "That's what happens when you dig holes in lawns!"

Bailey wagged his tail. Copper

wriggled between her legs.

"People don't like it!" Ella explained.
"They so-o-o-o don't like it, do they,
Dad?"

Have you read...

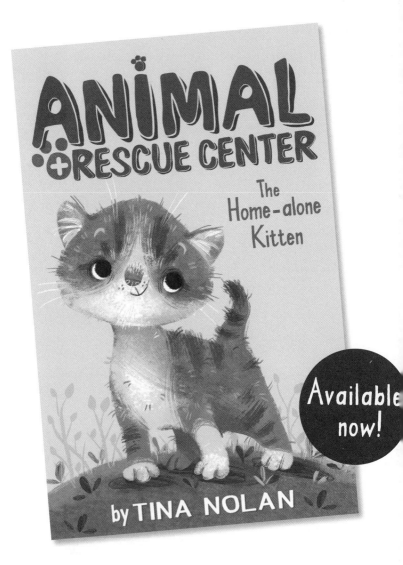

ANIMAL RESCUE CENTER

The Home-alone Kitten

Available now!

by TINA NOLAN

Abandoned ... lost ... neglected?
There's always a home
at Animal Magic!

In a perfect world, there would be no need for
Animal Magic. But Ella and Caleb Harrison,
who live at the animal rescue center with their
parents, know that life isn't perfect. Every day
there's a new arrival in need of their help!

When soccer star Jake Adams cancels his appearance
at Animal Magic's anniversary celebration, Ella is
determined to find out why. But when she and Caleb
arrive at Jake's house, all they find is his adopted
kitten, Charlie, meowing on the doorstep....

Have you read...

ANIMAL RESCUE CENTER

The Injured Fox Kit

Available now!

by TINA NOLAN